BIG FRIENDS

Margery Cuyler

Illustrations by Ezra Tucker

Walker & Company ✸ New York

To Al and Julia, magnificent friends —M. C.

For my very patient and loving wife, Nancy,
and children, Noël, Nelson, and Maclin —E. T.

First published in the United States of America in 2004 by
Walker Publishing Company, Inc.

Published simultaneously in Canada by Fitzhenry and Whiteside, Markham, Ontario L3R 4T8

For information about permission to reproduce selections from this book, write to Permissions,
Walker & Company, 104 Fifth Avenue, New York, New York 10011

Library of Congress Cataloging-in-Publication Data

Cuyler, Margery.
Big friends / Margery Cuyler ; illustrations by Ezra Tucker.
p. cm.
Summary: Big Hasuni, a lonely giant, accidentally makes a mess when he goes to an island to investigate the
smoke he has seen there, then returns home to find that someone has done the same thing to his mountain home.
ISBN 0-8027-8886-6 (hc) – ISBN 0-8027-8887-4 (re)
[1. Giants—Fiction. 2. Loneliness—Fiction. 3. Friendship—Fiction.] I. Tucker, Ezra N., ill. II. Title.
PZ7.C997Bh 2004
[E]—dc22
2003057176

The artist used acrylic paint and gouache on gessoed hot-press illustration board
to create the illustrations for this book.

Book design by Victoria Allen

Visit Walker & Company's Web site at www.walkeryoungreaders.com

Printed in Hong Kong

2 4 6 8 10 9 7 5 3 1

Up above and far away,

Big Hasuni lived on top of a great big mountain. He had no son or daughter. He had no wife or mother. Instead he had two pets, a lion and an elephant. And although they were his friends, he sometimes felt very lonely.

One morning, while Big Hasuni was making porridge in his cooking pot, he looked out at the view. He could see the trees of the deep dark forest, the waters of the clear blue lake, the grass of the wide open plain, and the sands of the vast scorching desert. And down below and far away, he gazed at the small island in the middle of the great big ocean.

But today something was different. A plume of smoke, as soft and thin as a feather, was rising above the island.

Big Hasuni was so excited, he dropped his cooking spoon. He called to the lion and the elephant, "Let's hurry down the mountain and find out what's making that smoke."

So off they went without even eating their breakfast. They trotted down the great big mountain, through the deep dark forest, around the clear blue lake, across the wide open plain, and over the vast scorching desert until they came to the great big ocean.

Big Hasuni didn't waste any time. He waded through the water until he reached the island's sandy shores.

A trail of footprints, each the size of a baobab tree, led through the sand. Big Hasuni, the lion, and the elephant followed the footprints up, up, up to a clearing. In the clearing, they saw a big hammock, an old rickety stool, and a campfire with a dozen giant lobsters steaming in a nest of seaweed.

"YUM, YUM, YUM," said Big Hasuni, whose stomach was growling after his long hike without any breakfast. No one seemed to be around, so he gobbled up all the lobsters.

When he had finished eating, Big Hasuni sat down on the stool to have a rest. The stool was so old and rickety, it broke! Big Hasuni fell to the ground, *KABOOM!* The island shook, causing a tidal wave, and some of the leaves fell from the palm trees.

"*OUCH!*" said Big Hasuni. He stood up and rubbed his sore bottom.

Then he let out a yawn and
gazed at the big hammock.
It looked so comfortable that
he lay down. As the wind
gently rocked him, he fell into
a deep, snory sleep.

After a while, a giant woman with a face as round as a full moon and a hat the color of cherries came lumbering into the campsite.

"Sour lemongrass!" she cried when she saw the lobster shells scattered on the ground.

"Clicking tortoise shells!" she exclaimed when she saw the broken stool.

"Jumping tuna!" she yelled when she saw the hammock with a man the size of a giant in it.

She swung the big hammock so hard that Big Hasuni fell out and hit the ground for a second time. *OUCH!* Big Hasuni's eyes snapped open. He was so startled that he leaped up and started to run.

"Wait!" yelled the giant woman.

But Big Hasuni, the lion, and the elephant had already reached the great big ocean. They waded through the water and ran back over the vast scorching desert, across the wide open plains,

around the clear blue lake, through the deep dark forest, and up the great big mountain. They ran all the way to Big Hasuni's campsite, where they found . . .

a DISASTER!

Big Hasuni's campsite was topsy-turvy. The giant's wooden stool was broken into a hundred pieces. His hammock was twisted into a big knot. And his cooking pot was lying upside down.

"Bouncing boulders!" cried Big Hasuni. "Who has destroyed my campsite?"

Just then, the giant woman with a face as round as a full moon and a hat the color of cherries came lumbering up the great big mountain. She stopped and pointed a finger at Big Hasuni.

"Well?" she said.

"Well?" said Big Hasuni.

"Did you make that mess down below?" she asked.

"Did you make this mess up above?" he asked.

"I wanted to see what was making the smoke on top of the mountain," she said.

"I wanted to see what was making the smoke below on the island," he said.

A low laugh started in the throat of the giant woman.

A low laugh started in the throat of the giant man.

"My name is Big Hanna," she said. "And I'm sorry I made such a mess of your mountain."

"My name is Big Hasuni," he said. "And I'm sorry I made such a mess of your island."

Soon they were laughing and bellowing, making the mountain shake and the clouds jump in the sky.

Finally Big Hasuni said, "Do you want
some dinner?"

Big Hanna answered, "Do you want
some company?"

They both nodded and smiled. Big Hasuni
put the stool back together and fixed the
hammock. Big Hanna built a fire
and roasted some meat.

Soon they were all eating dinner.

And that's how the giant up above and the
giant down below finally became big friends.

And so ends my story.